Also From Jisa

Lake House
Lakeside daddy
Down by the Lake
Lakefront Property
Back to the Lake

Booked
Overdue
Late Notice

Blue Venus
Crimson Deep
Violet Ends

Urgent Care
Code blue
Under New Management

Dark Redemption
Going Dark
Black Site
Outside the Wire
Code Bravo

Poe

Taboo Series:
Quarantine Bunny
You Bet
For Hire
Too Intense
For Love
Dangerous Seduction
Double the Pleasure
PussyCat
Sir Richard's Portait
Half Cocked
Who Wants Pie

Stand Alones:
Bewitched
Melt For me
Burn for me
Stocking stuffer
All the Trimmings
Hard Candy
Blind Love
In His Custody

The Animal Within
The Monster Inside
The Human Between
The Peace Within
Rule of the Animals

Beneath the Calm
Below the Surface

Hauntingly Ever After
Frightening Desires
Pumkin Kisses
Baby Gravy
All Wrapped Up
Midnight Kisses
Provocative
Ghost of a Chance
Spreading Joy
Saving Christmas
Tangled in Tinsel
Lucky Charm

Something Borrowed
Something Blue
Something Old
Something New
Something More
Starting Something

Under My Tree
New Release
Never Say Never

Always
Heartthrob

No part of this publication may be reproduced, distributed, or transmitted in any form or by any means, including photocopying, recording or other electronic or mechanical methods, without prior written permission of the author, except in the case of breif quotations embodied in critical reviews and certain other noncommercial uses permitted by copyreightlaw. For permission requests, email:

jisadean@yahoo.com

http://www.jisadean.com

Publisher's Note: This is a work of fiction. Names, characters, places, and incidents are a product of the author's imagination. Locals and public names are sometimes used for atmospheric purposes. Any resemblance to actual people, living or dead, or to buisness, companies, events institutions, or locals is completely coincidental.

Copyright © 2020 by Author Jisa Dean

All rights reserved.

ISBN:9798391126089

YouBet

Lacie's in a bad situation. She has been offered as ante in a poker game by her stepfather to one of his rich over-indulged friends and it's not to do something as mundane as cleaning his house. When she meets Erik, he is anything other than what she is expecting. Not only is he sexy and the chemistry between the two of them is off the charts but he is just as p$*#ed at her stepfather as she is. He wants to be more than just her friend though. He wants to take care of her and make her his. Is she ready for a way older guy to take care of her every wish or will the shattered trust her stepfather left her with bring a good thing to an end?

This is book two of my Taboo series. The trope heavy slightly dubious love story that has a guaranteed Happily Ever After is sure to leave you hot and bothered and glad it only takes one hand to turn the page. It's a standalone that doesn't have to be read with any of the others and doesn't necessarily interact with any of the other stories in the series. Come to the dark side and find out what makes us love these naughty tropes so much!

You Bet

Taboo Series: Book Two

JISA DEAN

Chapter 1

Erik

I see Brad pull up and heft out a loud sigh. I didn't want him to actually follow through with our little bet. I was hoping when I got home today that I would have a nice, quiet, relaxing afternoon where I didn't have to worry about other people's bullshit. Seeing Brad's tiny ass Prius tells me that's not going to happen. Now I have to gauge how quickly I can get rid of him and his daughter.

There's no way in hell I'm going through with this bet. Especially not when Brad's big selling point is how good of a lay his daughter is. Well, stepdaughter, which doesn't make it any less tolerable for me. I have plenty of time to think back over how I got myself into this mess. Four days ago I'm enjoying a high-end poker game with some people in the higher circles of society. Enjoy might be putting too positive a spin on it. I tolerated being there for business purposes. When you are successful and bored you'd be surprised at the shit you can find to be a part of.

Not me, per se. I actually have a momma at home that would kill me if she found out some of the shit that these guys are up to. But the other guys think nothing of trading wives and cars and homes like they are kids exchanging baseball cards. Still, I make an appearance every now and then to make sure I have an eye on the competition. I didn't make my money by sitting on the sidelines wondering what these people have in their closets. I make it a priority to find every dirty thing about the people I do business with. You never know when a dead hooker or a live schoolgirl is going to pop up and make someone give you what you want without all the hassle.

Most of the entertainment I go to isn't as seedy as the one I was in a couple of nights ago but I got a call from an old friend and he wanted to meet at the party. I'm at this poker game going from table to table with a room full of wealthy, bored men. Naked women are floating around offering drinks and anything else someone might take a liking to if they pay enough when I finally meet up with Brad. He's not from money and he'sno good at making or keeping it so the fact that he was at this game was a little shocking.

Apparently, he had come into some money because his wife passed away and left him with some. Again Brad can't hang on to money for shit but I was willing to give him a few hours. We went to college together, both on scholarships because we weren't part of the rich boy fraternity that ran the school. It had been years since I'd seen him and he hit me up at a moment of weakness when I didn't have anything else to do. It didn't hurt that one of the men I wanted to do some work with was also going to be there.

Despite Brad's shitty luck in the monetary category that night he was actually doing pretty decent. He had won several of the smaller tables and was allowed into the big one with guys like me. My future business partner had left to get his dick sucked by the blonde waitress he had been flirting with all night. So I was about to call it a night when it was down to just me, Brad, and one other guy with a handlebar mustache and a heavy drinking problem. This really was a shitty place.

The pot was big and getting bigger but then

right at the end of the game, Brad didn't have enough funds to cover the ante. I told him I would spot him some cash but he wouldn't hear of it. Instead, the dumb son of a bitch started talking about his daughter, stepdaughter, and about what a hot little piece she was. How she could suck a dick like a Hoover and still be able to get you hard after. I was so close to backing out and telling him what a piece of shit he'd turned into until something he said caught my attention. The girl had just turned eighteen - like a couple of days ago and had finished high school two weeks before that.

Handlebar was all for him some young tail and agreed to make her part of the wager. The way Brad worded it was shady as fuck too - a 'date' with his daughter. The asshole even used air quotes when he was talking about it. This girl was young, hell it had been nearly fifteen years since I was twenty which was a lot closer to eighteen than I am now. I stayed in thinking if I won I would at least take the kid out for dinner and let her have a break from all the dick-sucking Brad apparently made her do. Who knows how many times Brad's put her in the pot so to speak?

Turns out Handlebar and Brad suck at Poker. Brad leans over and gives me a lecherous smile that makes me want to take a shower and tells me he's really happy it's me who's gonna have a shot at her. I've been trying for the last four days to tell him to fuck off and that I have no intentions of fucking his stepdaughter. Especially not since I won her in a goddamn poker game.

He would have probably brought her here the next day but I had to fly out to take care of some business in Europe. I'm tired, I'm jet-lagged, and I just want peace, not a Hoover. Still, here I am standing at the living room window watching my idiot friend bring his stepdaughter to me. I let Dasha answer the door. Dasha has been with me for many years now and she has a small cabin set some ways away from the house but still on my property where she lives with her husband. My mom comes over to talk to Dasha more than she does me sometimes. Not that I have the time to just sit and talk anyway.

Dasha comes to the door of the living room followed by Brad and who I can only assume is his daughter. She doesn't look eighteen. She doesn't look like she can suck anything other than a milkshake either. She's practically a baby. I run my hand down my face and try to control myself. Dasha looks as concerned as I am. I feel like a perv for even thinking she's attractive. Something about Brad's story isn't adding up.

One of the most glaring things about this whole mess is I think this girl has been drugged because she looks glassy-eyed and when Dasha tells her to sit down it takes her a while to actually sit. Brad has to take her by the hand and pull her down on the couch beside him. When I turn my stare back on him he's all smiles like this is a normal social visit between two old friends.

Thank God the girl isn't dressed like she is going to a kink party right after this. She's in blue jean shorts and a tank top with a cartoon character on it. Silence fills the room for a good minute and a half before Brad finally breaks it by looking at the kid sitting next to him and elbowing her.

"This is my friend Erik. Say hi, Lacie." When the girl doesn't say anything he pushes her up on her feet and shoves her toward me. When I catch her she gasps out, really the only response I've seen from the girl since she's walked in. "So you want me to wait down here or…I could wait in the car if you wanted to do it right here."

The girl's, Lacie's, body doesn't feel like a kid's body. Her breasts are pushed into my chest and I can tell by the hold I have on her hips that she's curvy everywhere. And I'm back to feeling like a perv again. Her eyes don't meet mine, instead looking down as she mumbles her hello.

"Brad, we've got to talk, man." There is no way I am giving her back to him. Not like this. Who knows where he could take her?

"Oh, you're worried about knocking her up. Don't be. She's on birth control. I take her to get them every month so I know she's good."

Jesus, Brad is a real cunt! I have to get to the bottom of this whole mess before I let this girl go anywhere with anyone else. I can tell by how hard she is leaning into me that she's definitely on something. I'm practically holding her up now so she won't fall to the floor.

"I was going to tell you this was a bad idea but seeing her," I try to sit down with her and fumble for a split second on how I can keep her close and propped up enough that she looks like she will participate. If she's too out of it he might 'postpone' tonight. I finally settle on pulling her into my lap and rolling her head over so it looks like she might be nuzzling my neck. "I think I'm going to need a little bit more time with her. How about you give me all night and you can have her back, say tomorrow afternoon." It will take my lawyers that long to alert the proper authorities to what Brad is doing.

Brad looks like he just won the god damned Super Bowl and if this girl is on birth control I'll eat my checkbook. He bounces up, nodding and grinning. "That sounds good. You did win her fair and squareafter all. I never said how long the date had to be so it's only fair that you get your money's worth out of her."

I hear what may be a little whimper coming from the girl in my lap at his words. Sweet Jesus this isn't right. Dasha shows him out and I can tell by her pinched face she'snot happy with any of this. As soon as he's through the door I'm checking her vitals to make sure she's alright. Her pulse is slow but steady when I check.

She's beautiful. Dark soft hair, soulful eyes, thick soft lips, and on second glance she doesn't look like a kid either. She's got nice full breasts that bounce when I move her letting me know she'snot wearing a bra. Her ass is sweet and round sitting on my lap like she is. I can't fight my body's response to her as my dick gets hard under her.

Her worried eyes make it go down faster than if my mother walked in on me. "Sorry." I'm about to tell her she doesn't have anything to worry about when we're interrupted.

"You are not touching that girl!" Dasha says as she comes back into the room from escorting Brad out. Her eyes are shooting sparks and she is standing like she is ready to fight all the demons in hell to keep my girl safe. She really needs a raise. And did I just call this girl 'mine'? What the hell is up with that?

"Of course I'm not! What do you think I am, a monster? I couldn't give her back to him either. Who knows what he would have done with her?"

Her mouth pops open in a shocked 'o' and I can tell poor Dasha didn't think about that. I scoop my girl up in my arms and carry her to the stairs right outside the living room door. Dasha trails after me.

"Call the doctor and tell him I'll pay him extra if he gets over here ASAP."

She gives me a nod and runs to do as I say. I make quick work of the stairs and take my new responsibility to my bedroom.

"No one's going to hurt you here, Lacie, okay." Her name is even sweet and delicate. It fits her. "Can you tell me how you came to be here with us?"

"Brad...," she closes her eyes right after she whispers it.

"Did he hurt you?" when I don't get a response I jiggle her a little bit and pull her face back to mine. "Lacie, baby, did he hurt you?"

She has tears in her eyes when she looks back at me but she shakes her head slowly. But something inside is eating away at me. I go to the door and lock it. I know we don't have a lot of time before Dasha is knocking the door down to make sure she is alright.

"Lacie, can I make sure he didn't hurt you?" her brows furrow at my question but after a moment she nods. I run my hands up her torso until I touch the bottom of her breasts and she sucks in a breath at my touch. I try to be clinical about making sure she doesn't have any bruises or wounds on her body but I don't think I am fooling anybody with the tent I am pitching in my dress pants.

When I pull her shirt up to her chin I can take in all of her creamy skin and how her hard little nipples furl in the cool air. I have to run my hand down my face again to remind myself this girl is here because of some sick bastard and he might have done more than drugged her. I roll her over so I can look at her back and see a small bruise on her lower back that looks like it might have come from a needle. I run my hands over it causing her to shiver.

I pull her shirt down and try to rearrange her so she doesn't look like someone mauled her. I turn her face back to mine. "Lacie, I'm going to ask you a question, baby, and I want you to answer it truthfully." Even though her eyes are glassy she gives me a little nod. "Are you a virgin?"

If I find out that mother fucker did something to her I won't have to call doctors and lawyers to go after him. I'll kill him myself. Her cheeks pinken and after a while, she nods her head yes.

"Lacie, I don't want the doctor checking but I need to know you've not been hurt. Can I look?"

Her brows crash together and fear swirls in her eyes and I can tell just like Dasha she didn't think of something so bad happening. She nods quickly this time giving me permission but doesn't say anything. I have my hands on the button of her shorts before she can stop nodding. I pull them down and see tiny black lace panties wrapped around a bare pussy. Her scent hits me and it's all I can do to hold back the moan wanting to come out.

I stop when she whimpers and shifts her legs. "You want me to stop and wait for the doctor?" her bottom lip is trembling and after more time she finally shakes her head no. She shocks me by spreading her legs more. I hook my hands in the sides of her panties and slowly slide them down her legs. There are times in a man's life when he can stand back and just know that life will never be the same. Seeing Lacie's pussy is one of those life-changing events.

She's bare so I can see all of her. Sweet little lips, just as plump as the ones on her face, wait for me to pull them open. I run my hand over my face and brace myself. I take a hand and spread her apart so I can look at the pink heart of her sex. She's fucking gorgeous. She probably has the prettiest pussy I have ever seen. When I look back at her, her cheeks are bright red and she whispers, "Just do it." But she never meets my eyes.

I realize I am breathing just as hard as she is and my hands are trembling when I run a finger up the soft folds. "I can't just shove it in, baby. That's going to hurt you more. I need you to relax and just...let me go slow."

I'm such a bastard. I'm sure I could just poke around until I confirm she still has her hymen without taking permanent mental images that will repeat in my head every time I want to whack off from now until the day I die. I run my finger up her folds again and stop when she tenses up and a moan falls out of her mouth. I immediately give her my eyes. She rolls her head so she doesn't have to look at me.

"I can't stop them from coming out. Feels good." Another moan leaves her lips as I keep rubbing her pussy until my fingers come away soaked.

"Shh, it's okay, baby. This is good. It means you're relaxing for me so I can check." She nods and gives me a whispered oh.

I finally run my finger back down until I am at her entrance. She's tight and even though she's wet I still can't get my finger to slip in. I need her to relax more. I grab her breast and give a tug to her nipple causing her to writhe on the bed and her body to shudder under my hands. As far as distractions go it is a good one because finally, I'm able to breach her virgin hole with my finger.

Her hand flies down to stop me, her fingers wrapped around my wrist making me stop even if there is no force there. Her body shakes and I realize when she starts to squeeze up around my finger that she is about to cum. Her eyes look scared and confused and I wonder if this is her first time cumming.

"Shh, don't be afraid, Lacie. Let it come.

No one has to know what happens in here between you and me." I keep talking to her right through her orgasm. Her body tenses and her eyes roll back until the tension inside of her snaps and her pussy gushes around my finger which I might have been rocking back and forth inside of her to help her find her release. I don't wait for her to realize what happened before I push further inside and touch the thin film of her barrier. She's still got her cherry…for now.

I pull my finger from her drenched little hole and I can't help myself from bringing my finger up to my mouth and sucking her off of it. Her eyes widen at what I am doing.

"You still have your cherry and your little pussy doesn't look like it's been hurt. But Lacie," I wait until she looks into my eyes before I continue, "you belong to me now. You're mine. Do you understand?"

Before I can get an answer from her there is a loud bang on the door that makes Lacie jump. I pull her panties and her shorts back up and fasten them before I go over to the door and unlock it. Dasha is standing on the other side looking mad as hell.

"You better not have done anything to that child!"

Chapter 2

Lacie

I hear people talking around me but I can't make out what they are saying. The last thing I remember is I was at my stepdad's house arguing with him about money. It's always been about money for him. I think that's one of the reasons he married my mom because she had a small fortune from when my dad died. We could have been well off for life if had she never met Brad.

Brad saw this lonely, hurting widow and spent the time it took to sweep her off her feet but it was all a lie. She was beginning to wise up to his ways at the end and would have probably divorced him if she hadn't gotten into a car crash and died leaving me with him. I wasn't quite eighteen yet. I still had a year to go and nowhere else to live. I knew mom had an insurance policy that went to me when I turned eighteen so I just had to bide my time.

One of the things Brad and I were arguing about

was him trying to get his greedy hands on the insurance money my mom left me. That money was my ticket out of there though and I wasn't helping anyone out with anything. Brad was an adult and was going to have to make his own way in life without the help of me or my mom ever again. He told me he had a guaranteed way for us to make some money and proceeded to tell me about this scam to honeytrap one of his wealthy friends. He literally wanted to sell me to him for a night so the guy could knock me up and we would have money coming in every month.

He was becoming more and more insistent and I was terrified of what he might do. I was packing when he came in and he pretended like he was going to let me go and that he hated that we couldn't be closer. He must have snuck up on me while my back was turned with something because the next thing I knew I was dizzy and my arms and legs weren't moving like they were supposed to. He shoved me in the car and took off before I could figure out what was going on. When we pulled into the 'compound' I was so scared I thought my heart was going to beat out of my chest. He's going to force me to do something awful with someone I don't know - a 'friend' of his. Who knows what kind of vile person would agree to this kind of thing.

I started trying to fight through the drugs he gave me. Hard. Something must have given me away because when he realized it, he gave me more and there was no fighting after that. I don't remember much after that. Just fleeting images and a voice that was deep and soothing telling me no one was going to hurt me. I'm not sure if it was all in my head or if God sent an angel down to save me from Brad but it gave me the comfort I needed to let myself drift off to sleep.

"You should get some rest. I can sit with her. Tomorrow is going to be a hard day." A woman's soft voice drifts to me. It's heavy with some kind of accent but I can't tell what kind.

"No, you go on to bed. I'll take care of her." That's the voice! The one that made me feel so safe and cared for. Snippets of memory float back to me but they're fuzzy and I'm not sure if they are a dream or real. This tall, blue-eyed man standing over me playing with my body and making me feel good is one of my favorites. That one has to be a dream because I've never even been kissed so I know that one didn't happen. My friends all call me the prude. I don't much care. I've never met anyone I want to give my trust to enough for them to be close to me.

"She better not be any different than she is right now, Erik...," shit the rest of his name fades out before I can catch it all. I don't have a clue who Erik is or why he makes me feel so safe but he has the most amazing voice I've ever heard.

"And if she was? I've already told you how things are going to be from now on. She belongs to me, Dasha. I will do with her what I want when I want." That doesn't sound good. The voice takes on a hard edge that kind of reminds me of kings or lords declaring something so. The woman was just concerned about me.

I try to open my eyes but I can't get them unglued enough. Hands hold me down and force me to be still. More flashes of memory come to me, this man, Erik touching me, spreading my thighs so he can look at my pussy, and then popping his finger in his mouth after he's played with me. The memory makes me itchy or restless.

"It's the worst case I have seen in a while. He must have really been shooting her full of the stuff to have her like this." A new male voice makes my heart start beating harder. I can't bring myself to wake up or move for that matter. What's going to happen to me? Who is going to be around me when I'm this vulnerable and weak?

"But what was it and is it going to have any adverse effects on her afterward?" There is the man who saved me. Maybe it won't be bad if he's here.

"No, it shouldn't have any lasting effects. I'll have to take the blood work back to the lab to be sure of what it is but I don't think he wanted her dead or ill, he just wanted her compliant or at least to appear that way."

Oh my God! They're talking about the shit Brad gave me. I try hard to make myself wake up this time, wanting to tell them what happened and who Brad really is but it's so hard.

"And you said you did look her over for any signs of violence or assault and couldn't find any?"

"Nothing other than the needle mark on her back."

I pull my eyes open just barely and start trying to speak. The man with beautiful eyes is the first to notice and he goes still before bending closer to me so he can try to understand what I am telling him.

"Brad...," I want to say so much. I want to tell him what he's done but when I think about everything all I can think about is throwing up. And that's exactly what happens in the seconds following Brad's name.

The man whose voice is so soothing to me grabs me up and helps me lean over the bed so I can hit a trashcan instead of the pillow beside my head. He holds me and makes sure my hair doesn't fall into my face.

"Well, this is a good thing."

The man holding me turns to look at the other man in the room and gives him a what-the-fuck look.

"Her body is trying to get rid of what he put in it. As long as she doesn't choke on her vomit it's a good thing." The man doesn't leave my side but he shouts the roof down for someone named Dasha. "I'll run these over to the lab and make sure they understand they are to be done on the double. By tomorrow at noon, we should know more."

"Remember the other thing we talked about. If you can tell me anything let me know."

The doctor nods and then leaves as a stunning blonde walks in with worried blue eyes. She's beautiful too. Just like the man who is holding me. Maybe I died and these are my parents in heaven or something. I feel really shitty for this to be heaven. Shouldn't I feel better than I do? Maybe I got away and crawled to the nearest house to find help and they are the couple that is helping me.

The blonde busies herself getting things cleaned up so the man can sit with me. I really hope she's not his wife or girlfriend because I shouldn't be having dirty dreams about another woman's man. Maybe I shouldn't think about how this man makes me feel or think about all the dirty things I want him to do to me.

He brushes my hair back from my face. "Don't try to fight the sleep, baby. Just let it take you over. You're safe now. Nothing will ever hurt you again."

Yeah, this has to be the way into heaven. Because never having to worry about being hurt sounds damn good to me.

Chapter 3

Erik

I sit by her bedside and wait. My lawyers have already woke a judge up in the middle of the night and my investigators are working on finding out who the girl lying in my bed really is. By morning we should be set to grab Brad before he gets to the house. In fact, I might tell them to go ahead and have him arrested. The only reason I'm not is that my guys need time to work.

Lacie stirs in her sleep and makes me very aware of the fact that she is in my bed naked. I took her shirt off when she started throwing up. I'm glad she's getting whatever the hell she was given out but it seems violent when she does it. Thankfully she only did it a couple of times. I took her shorts off to make her more comfortable while she slept so the only thing she had on was a pair of wet black, lace panties. I couldn't leave her in those so I took those off too. She's completely bare under my sheets. Several times during the night I've run my hand up under the sheet to feel her satiny skin. Not to take what she's not awake to give but just to run my palm over her leg or down her arm.

Her eyes open and I can tell she is more at herself. They're not dulled by drugs or glassy with confusion anymore. "I thought I dreamed you into existence."

"I'm real, very, very real. How are you feeling?"

"Better." She spends a few minutes thinking about something before telling me what's on her mind, "I think I threw up on you."

I nod, making her groan, and look away. My phone rings in my pocket halting me from doing anything else to her. I look at it and realize it's the doctor. "I have to take this, baby. Don't move."

I step out of the room but I don't close the door. I don't wait on greetings before I am asking him questions about her results and whether or not the sweet thing in my bed is on anything.

"Wow, you really want to know what I found, huh." We go over what he sent to the police about the drugs she was given. One of my friends from the station already called me and told me to expect them to come by and take statements from all of us sometime in the afternoon if Lacie was feeling up to it. What he says next has my dick going hard like steel.

"Erik, if she's on anything, it's not any kind of birth control I've ever seen before. In fact, looking at her blood work I would say she's about to start ovulating in the next few days."

I let what he says sink in before I ask for clarification. "So you're telling me she's fertile."

"Well, yes, I guess you could put it that way. I prefer to say she's ovulating. It's a lot less like you are about to plant her in the ground but to each their own."

"You're saying she's ripe, yes or no?"

"Uh, yes. That would be a big capital 'Y' on that too. Although ripe is even worse than fertile."

I look back into the room where she is lying, her wide eyes taking in everything in the room. Brad might have lied about the birth control to get me to fuck a baby into his stepdaughter but he wasn't far off from what was going to happen. There is no way I'm letting Lacie go and the surest way to tie her to me is to knock her little ass up.

I thank the doctor and promise a hefty donation to his practice. I am back inside with her in seconds. I move to the bed and instead of sitting in the chair like before and I sit right beside her. "Lacie, baby, your...," I stop myself from calling him her father, "Brad told me you were taking birth control but the doctor couldn't find any in your blood work when he tested your hormones. Are you taking anything?"

She swallows hard and her brows draw together, her little nose scrunching up trying to figure out why Brad would lie about something like that. "I...I've never been on birth control. I don't, um...I've never needed it before."

"Yes, I am very aware that you kept that sweet cherry safely tucked away and that you might not have a reason to be on it for that but I had to ask." Her eyes widen at the memory I cause her to recall from last evening. "So he never took you to get the shot?"

She shakes her head no, "Why would he lie about that?" her brows are drawn inward and I can spot the confusion swirling in her eyes. Such innocent eyes.

"Probably so when I fuck you, you would become pregnant with my baby and he could profit off of it." Her face goes ashen at my words.

"He told me about a 'plan' of his that would make us both money, you're the man he was talking about aren't you?" She fills me in on the 'plan' Brad had cooked up.

I nod.

"I'm so sorry. I didn't have anything to do with this. Your wife must be so upset about all of this."

Now it's my turn to not understand. "What wife? I'm not married."

"Oh, I…thought the blonde woman…maybe I dreamed her."

"Oh, that's Dasha. She's not my wife. She's my housekeeper. Her husband is quite possessive of her actually. I never really understood until recently why he would lose his

mind anytime another man came around her but I am beginning to understand now. He is my driver and groundskeeper."

"Um, what happens next? I...," she looks up at me with worry and fear in her eyes. "I don't really have anywhere else to go and I definitely don't want to go back to Brad's." She plucks at the blanket not looking me in the eyes. "I have money from my mom I just have to wait to get it."

"Your inheritance?" she nods and the weight of the words I am about to say push down on me. "Baby, Brad got his hands on that money. It's not there anymore."

I keep talking, telling her that we think he might have forged her signature but she's not listening to me. She doesn't look up and I swear I can see the glimmer of tears on her lashes. "Can I be alone for a little while, please?"

I take her chin and raise her head so I can look at her. Her tears leave tracks down her cheeks and break my heart. "You're right. You can't go back to Brad's. He'll just try to do this again and again until he eventually succeeds." I hate to tell her but I want her to know what will happen if she doesn't take what I am offering her. "That's why you will stay here. In my house, until we find out what is going on and what the next step is."

"I can't. I have some friends I can stay with...,"

"No! The police are coming to take statements and it would be easier and better for everyone if they didn't have to waste resources and effort in trying to find you as you couch surf from one friend to the next. Not to mention right now is the time Brad is the most dangerous, none of your friends have the kind of security and protection I do."

"Dangerous?" her eyes question me and I see the flash of fear in them. It makes me want to kill someone - preferably Brad.

"He's looking at quite a few charges against him, not the least of which being drugging you and bringing you here to try to solicit sex when you clearly didn't know or want to do what he was making you do, stealing your inheritance, and forging signatures that helped him commit fraud. He is looking at a very harsh punishment. That makes men like him dangerous to the people attacking him."

"But I'm not the one attacking him. I didn't start any of this."

"No, you didn't but someone like Brad doesn't understand that. He just sees that he got in trouble because of something he did to you and he'll want to blame someone for that. It doesn't matter one way or another, you are staying here, end of discussion. Now rest while you can."

Chapter 4

Lacie

When I open my eyes again the pretty blonde woman is sitting by my bed. I think she might be knitting, which seems odd for someone as pretty as she is to be doing something I normally associate with my great-aunt. She doesn't realize that I am awake and it gives me the opportunity to look at her without her knowing. The light is casting a pretty golden glow on the woman and it makes me think of an angel. She has the face of a model, thin and ethereally beautiful. How is the man who was sitting with me last night, not with this woman?

I remember he said she had a husband. He must be fucking stunning if he is with this woman. Before I can drag my eyes away from her she is looking up at me. Her eyes are the clearest blue I have ever seen.

"Oh, you're awake. Good. He will be happy about

walking away from me, "I've found you some stretchy leggings of mine and he told me to give you this shirt. I do believe the police are still here. I will go tell Mr. Erik that you are awake."

She's gone so fast that I can't ask her any questions. The thought of the police being here makes my stomach roll. I know they are going to want to ask about what happened and I am going to have to tell them how stupid I was to turn my back on someone like Brad. At least I feel stupid for doing it. I slowly get out of bed and look at the clothes. I look around for my bra and panties but I can't find them.

After I put the clothes on I step out of the room hoping to find my way to the stairs. I look like I am a child dressed in adult clothing. The leggings aren't as tight as they should be and I had to roll them up at the bottom and the shirt hangs down to my knees. For a moment I thought about just wearing it and skipping the leggings altogether. It takes me a minute to find the stairs and when I come down, I find myself in an entryway so I have to figure out which way to go to get to where I am supposed to be.

Out of nowhere, the blonde pops up to take me by the hand. "This way." She walks me to a set of double doors before letting me go to open them. "Mr. Morgan, she's here."

Erik stands and walks to me, taking my hand to lead me to the couch he was sitting on. On the other side of a coffee table, two men sit in slacks and polos with the police emblem on the pocket. They stand until I sit. Erik introduces them as the two detectives that will be handling things.

"Why don't you tell us what happened, Ms. Ross? In your own words." I side-eye Erik a little, not really wanting him to find out how silly I was. But he surprises me by taking my hand in his and resting it on his thigh giving me support.

I go over my last hours with Brad, telling them about trying to pack to leave and about him injecting me with something by stabbing me in the back with a needle, at least I think that's what happened. I mention the plot he came up with to honeytrap someone into knocking me up, although that comes out reluctantly. The entire time I can feel Erik's eyes on me but he doesn't stop me or say anything.

When I'm done telling them everything I can, including the part where I didn't sign money over to him like the documents are showing, Erik stands and takes me by the hand.

"Thank you, Lacie. Why don't you have Dasha show you where the big bathtub is and you can have a nice relaxing soak. Gentlemen," he walks with me to the doors where Dasha is standing. Before turning back he cups my cheek with his palm. "I will be up to see you soon."

I don't really want to analyze his comment too much. If he wants me to take a bath then why would he be up soon to see me? Wouldn't I still be in the bathroom? Maybe it is just something he says like see you later or talk to you soon. I follow Dasha out of the room and up the stairs back to the room I was in last night. She leads me to a closed door on the left side of the room. When she pushes the door open I can see the bathroom is like something out of a freaking movie set or a castle.

The walls are painted a pale, soft blue. There are arches leading into all the areas of the bathroom, the shower, the tub, and the vanities like something out of a Turkish bath.

Something that appears to be marble is covering the steps to the tub and the tub itself looks like it's made of the same stuff. The tub is huge. It could fit me and Dasha and still have room for Erik in it too.

Behind the tub is a rock shelf with lots of bottles. Dasha pulls some down and starts the water. When she pours from the bottle she's holding the smell of lavender and honeysuckle fills the room and bubbles start to build on the water. "Mr. Erik's mother stays over sometimes and uses the guest bathroom. I moved all of her scented things in here for you to use."

"Um, I don't want to take her things."

She bustles around the room, getting more towels, "Nonsense, she won't mind and Mr. Erik will be more than happy to replace whatever you need to use. The towels are here," she shows me where she puts them, "and your clean clothes are here. If there is anything you need just let me know. I will be up with a platter of fruit for you soon and something for you to drink as well. Please take your time and enjoy your bath." She seems like she is really happy to have someone to help. I wonder if it's just Erik most of the time and that is why she seems so pleased to do these things for me.

"Thank you. You really don't have to bother. I don't want to be any trouble."

"Oh don't you worry, it's no trouble. And if the look in Erik's eyes is any indication you are going to need to keep your appetite up." She looks at me and then giggles. I have no idea what she's talking about which is why I think she is laughing. She turns to leave but I swear she whispers something about not being able to wait to tell his mother. I have no idea what she is so excited about telling her. Maybe Erik doesn't get very many guests and they're excited about having someone stay. Maybe they don't get a lot of excitement and all of this drama I drug in with me is something they can talk about. Who knows.

I pull the clothes off and fold them before I get in. The tub is only half full and still running. As I sink down into the bubbles and hot water I take a moment to stop thinking about anything other than what I am doing right at this moment. It's been a long time since I felt this safe. Before my mom passed even. The whole bathroom smells so good and the warm water calms a lot of the things going on in my head. I don't know how long I have sat just enjoying the quiet when I hear the door creak open.

My eyes pop open but then I remember Dasha saying she would be coming back with food so I don't freak out as much as I probably should've. I hear her set down the tray of food behind me but she doesn't leave like I thought she would. "Everything okay?"

Large hands land on my shoulders moments before a very deep, very un-Dasha voice speaks to me, "Everything is absolutely wonderful now."

I sit up and whirl to look at him. He lets me go but doesn't back up or turn to give me privacy. My arms come up to cover my boobs and I look down to make sure the bubbles are still covering my lap. Some of them have disappeared but it's still hard to make out what is underneaththem so I just worry about keeping my boobs hidden. Not that he hasn't seen it all before but this time I am more at myself.

He kneels down and lets his fingertips dip down into the water. In his other hand is a piece of fruit. He holds it to my lips and waits for me to open my mouth and let him in. The flavor of the fruit bursts on my tongue and makes me moan. When I open my eyes I see the intense look Erik is giving me. He reaches for another piece of fruit without taking his eyes off me.

He doesn't look away as he watches my mouth bite into the flesh of the cantaloupe I am eating. I would be worried but that's the farthest thing from what I feel when I am around him. It's the oddest thing too because he's the man who won me in a poker game. I should be freaking out and yelling and screaming at him not to touch me. Erik is the first person besides my mom that makes me feel safe.

My eyes follow the fruit he is hoping up to his lips and I watch as his teeth sink into it before it disappears. I've never really been all that interested in boys or sex especially not after my mom found Brad. For the first time, I find myself oddly fascinated by someone. The hand he has been dangling into the water this entire time dips a little lower finding my knee under the bubbles.

I jump but he doesn't move it any higher.

"No need to be so worried or startled."

I find myself calming instantly for him.

"Tell me about your mother and father and how Brad got involved with your family."

"Dad died, and mom was lonely. She didn't date for years after but I think the older I got the more she started to feel even more alone." Which makes me indirectly responsible for Brad. If I had only been there for my mom more maybe she wouldn't have tried to find someone else - at least not when she did.

"You know you aren't responsible for any of the things that happened right."

That's nice for him to say to me but I don't really believe it. I wouldn't be here in the bath naked with a stranger if I was better at spotting Brad's kind or if I did something sooner to prevent it from happening. His hand moves higher on my thigh. He doesn't seem to think it is weird or inappropriate to be touching me so close. He just picks up another slice of fruit and holds it expectantly to my mouth.

He starts to squeeze my leg in something like a one-handed massage. It feels nice and I forget that I am supposed to worry about keeping my boobs covered and not letting his hand climb any higher. Instead, I sink further down in the water and let him continue working my lax muscles over. He stands for a moment breaking my warm, little bubble.

"So skittish. Is that because of Brad or because you're a virgin?" He takes his shirt off as he asks and my eyes go wide.

"Wh...What are you doing?"

He walks behind me. "Just going to make you feel better, little one. You seemed to like what I was doing to your leg I thought you might like more of it."

His hands land on my shoulders and I moan at the first good squeeze. "I thought so." He sounds so sure of himself. "See, you did want more." My head lolls back as his strong hands work the knots out of my tense shoulders.

Once again all thoughts of hiding myself from him vanish. For the next little while, the only sounds in the bathroom are my moans and sighs as he rubs me. Then his hands go lower. Not at first but little by little they edge down. My nipples crinkle and harden the lower he goes. Soon he has his hands on the swell of my breasts. When I tilt my head back to look into his eyes he meets mine daring me to tell him to stop. I don't.

His hands move lower until his fingertips brush the edge of my areolas causing me to gasp. "Your body is very responsive."

What does that mean? "Thank you I guess."

"Your nipples are hard and I've barely even touched them. It makes me think you are more of a virgin than I first thought."

"Are there different ways to be a virgin? I mean pretty much if you're a virgin you're a virgin. Right?" I wait for him to agree with me but he doesn't. Instead, he dips his hands down lower until he is fully cupping my wet mounds.

"Oh, that answer specifically tells me how much you are actually a virgin. You can still be a virgin and let a boy touch you all over, fondle your breasts, touch you here." One of his hands dips under the water and cups my pussy causing me to squeal before I can slam my hands over my mouth. "You can still be a virgin if you allow them to give you an orgasm by rubbing you here."

His finger parts me and he finds the nub of sensational nerves that make my body tighten and makes me moan for him to keep going.

"You can be a virgin and technically have someone kiss you here," his finger finds my other hole and rubs against it, "and here. Hell, you can fuck here and still be considered a virgin." His finger presses in and I whine.

"But I think you haven't done any of those things with anyone have you?" His touch drifts back up to my clit and he starts stroking it again.

"I...you...no. Just the time you touched me yesterday." My voice comes out high and thin. I don't want to sound like a fool in front of him but I can't seem to act cool when his fingers are deftly building me up to a mind-blowing orgasm.

"Was that your first orgasm?" I nod my head in answer. "You ever play with yourself? Give yourself pleasure? Maybe sink a finger inside to find out what it feels like?"

I shake my head no. I wasn't really that curious before I met him.

"So my fingers are the only fingers that have

touched this pretty little pussy?"

Oh my God, there is no way I can answer him with words so I just nod again. Before I know what he is doing he has me up under the arms lifting me out of the tub and laying me on the floor. The cool tile contrasting with the heat of my bath and what he was doing to me.

"I'm going to put my mouth on you, Lacie, and eat the fuck out of this little fruit you've been keeping hidden away. You're going to tell me I can." When I don't say anything, because how could I after that he growls, "Tell me, Lacie."

I give him a quick nod. "I need words, Lacie. Give me fucking words."

"Oh God, please. You can do whatever you want to me."

"Fuck!" he's spread my legs with his wide shoulders before I can finish my sentence. His curse word is muffled by the puffy folds of my pussy. He uses his fingers to spread me wide so he can suck and feast on my clit. My voice is echoing off the tile and walls of the bathroom and my thighs are shaking around his head like I'm having a seizure.

This time when I cum I'm aware of what it feels like and I'm prepared to ride the wave over but he reaches up with his fingers and starts to play with my nipples as he's eating the cream from in between my legs. My body can't function when two spots are being made to feel so good. I plant my heels on his shoulders and ride his face, wild with need. My body tingles and then a warm wave of release pours over me from head to toe making me cry out as the muscles of my pussy flutter around his tongue.

When it's all over and I'm staring up at the bathroom ceiling waiting for shyness to creep back in but all I feel is bone-deep contentment. He drops a little kiss on top of my slick sex before he lifts me and lowers me back into the bath. All around his face is wet with traces of me. His tongue sweeps out licking around his lips and he moans. "So good. Now finish your bath so I can show you around the house and wine and dine you for dinner."

He kisses the top of my head before walking out and pulling the door closed, but it doesn't latch all the way. I'm starting to sink lower into the water and enjoy the post-orgasm high when I hear a voice that yanks me from it.

Brad.

Brad is here.

I slip out of the bath carefully since the floor is still really wet and reach for a towel. I just want to find out what is happening and if he is going to be arrested or not. I wrap the huge towel around me and make my way down the hall to a room with the door ajar a little.

When I hear Erik my heart stops. He's talking to my stepfather. Why? What is going on? I creep closer until I can hear what is being said

Chapter 3

Erik

"So where is she?" Brad has no idea how much I want to reach across the desk and kill him for what he's done to Lacie. As soon as he got here I made sure Dasha showed him to my office and offered him the scotch he was eye-fucking from across the room. I wonder if he has a drinking problem along with all the other faults he has or if he just craves expensive things.

"She is resting, after the night I gave her she needed her sleep." Brad laughs like I've made some grand joke that only he and I are privy to. He downs the glass and holds it out for more.

"Awesome, well I guess it's time to wake her up. I have to go meet a man about a boat this evening."

"I'm sorry Brad. She won't be going back with you."

"What?" at first his face goes as white as death

but then he flushes an angry shade of red. He puts the glass of half-full Scotch on my desk. I snarl my nose up at his lack of manners. "Stop playing you son of a bitch and give me my daughter."

"Step. Step-daughter. And I'm afraid she can't leave with you. See it occurred to me last night that you might have lied about her being on anything so I had her checked. She is now walking around with my baby in her belly and will not be leaving with you. Sorry, guess you're going to have to find another way to buy your boat. My child will not be one of those ways."

Fuck talking about Lacie being full of my kid is making it painfully uncomfortable to keep sitting. Brad jumps up and storms around the room. He opens his mouth a couple of times but can't find the words.

"That's fucking kidnapping. You can't just take a person, Erik."

"Oh but you can use them as ante in a poker game. You essentially sold her to me, is that not right?"

"Yeah, but that was different. That was for

one night. Hell, I even made sure she was good and wound up for you. She's not going to want to stay here once she...,"

"Once she what, Brad?"

"Once the stuff I gave her wears off."

I act shocked. "You gave her something?"

"Well, yeah. I kind of had to. She is high-spirited sometimes and I didn't want her to get the wrong idea and upset you. But you can't just have her. I need her back."

"Like you needed her mom's money?" He stops and looks at me with a worried frown on his face, the grooves deep in between his eyes. "I did a little digging."

"I needed that money to make sure we kept the apartment. It's not easy maintaining the kind of lifestyle Lacie is accustomed to and she owed that money to me."

"She was a child when you took it from her."

"Okay, okay. I see what kind of man I am working with. Let's make a deal of some kind. Let's come to an agreement like gentlemen." He leans forward and takes the glass back.

"I'm listening." The only deal I will be giving Brad is the one where he's either in jail or in the ground.

"You can keep her for a little longer and enjoy her some more and when the kid comes you can have it."

"And what do you get in return?"

"I want the money Lacie would have made me if she was doing this for other people. And I want to be compensated for the hassle of putting up with a pregnant girl. They can be so fucking moody." He's a disgusting little rodent and should be put down. The longer he talks the more I lean towards the shallow grave instead of the legal way of getting rid of him.

"And how will we get her to agree with this deal? Won't she want to keep the baby?"

"Oh, that won't be a problem when the time comes, we'll use the same stuff I used on her last night." The name of the drug falls from his lips and two armed men come into the room. They had been standing in the servants' nook this entire time but the wire I am wearing provided all the damning evidence they'll ever need to have to put him away.

My phone rings. I think about not taking it but it's my security team. "Gentlemen please excuse me. I'm confident you can take this trash out without my help. If there is anything you need simply ask for Dasha."

I answer and my heart drops at the first words. "Sir, she's on the move. She's about to leave the house...she's only wearing a towel, Sir." God damn it. I'm down the stairs and out the door before I can hang up with the head of my security. I tried to make sure Lacie was so stunned by the orgasm I gave her that she would stay put and never know Brad was here. I wore the wire because it was the only way I could make sure she wouldn't have to testify against him. The last thing I wanted was for her to be dragged into a courtroom with a jury and several journalists in the crowd. Not when I could handle it for her.

Something must've gone wrong and she overheard what was said or she took it the wrong way. Either way, I have to stop her before she leaves me. I have to bring her back inside the house before they pull Brad out and he sees what is mine. It's bad enough the security team has seen it. When I get my hands on her I am going to spank her hot little ass for going anywhere in a towel without me around.

I run down the front stairs of my house just as security pulls up in a big black SUV and cuts Lacie off from running through the yard and out of the gate. She comes up short and I have to say a prayer that the towel doesn't fall off of her. I must have made a sound, probably a growl, because she turns her head and our eyes clash. Hers swim in tears and a few drip off of her face killing me a little.

"Lacie, what the hell are you doing? Get back in the house?"

"No! You're just as bad as Brad. I heard what you said, what the two of you were talking about."

"God damn it, Lacie. Don't take another step or so help me...!" I have nothing really to supply with what I will do to her if she does other than spank her ass raw. I'm close enough to her now that I can almost reach out and grab her. She realizes it too because her eyes take on a wild look and I can tell she is going to try to make a run for it.

She takes off trying to skirt around the car but I am on her before she can so much as round the hood. I bend and flip her over my shoulder putting my hand on her ass to keep her towel from flipping up. Thank God I listened to Mom and invested in the big towels. I would have to kill half the men out here if not.

I make my way into the house and back upstairs to our bedroom. She wiggles and thrashes around the entire time. Halfway up the stairs, I give her ass a smack. No one is around now so I lift the towel until her naked cheeks are bared for me and then smack her again. She shrieks on my shoulder but goes still.

"I told you not to move or there would be consequences."

"I'm not a fucking child. I don't need my ass spanked."

The door to my office opens right as I top the stairs. I open one of the guest bedrooms and pull Lacie off my shoulder and into my arms covering her mouth so no one can hear her. The last thing I want is for these men to hear her say she doesn't want to stay here. I'm grateful I got her as far as I did before they came down the hall. Their footsteps are heavy and I wait for them to pass by the door before I grab Lacie around the waist and make a run for our bedroom. I fling her on the bed after I make sure the door is locked.

"You can't keep me here. That's kidnapping. I want to leave. NOW." She tries to move to the other side of the bed but I grab her ankle and pull her back. The towel is gone. It doesn't last after her trip across my bed. Once again I take her around the waist and this time pull her to the window.

"Look, god damn it!" I take her by the chin and force her to look out of the window we are standing at. In the driveway, the security team is still sitting there. The men have all gotten out and stand around talking to one of the detectives from earlier. The other detective and a police officer put a kicking Brad into the back of a police cruiser. My guys know the drill. They escort the police off the premises and the head of the security team goes with the detectives to talk about any footage and information we have on Brad. If they need me they will call me - after they call my lawyer of course.

Her little body goes lax in my hand. I can see her confusion written all over her face. "I don't understand."

"Which is the only reason I've not got you thrown over my lap spanking the hell out of you." I pull her back to the bed. This time when she falls back her hands try to cover her nakedness. Her arm bands across her breasts and the other hand cups her pussy.

She can tell where I am looking because I see her squirm, still so self-conscious about being bare in front of another person. Even though I have had my head between her legs. I reach up and start undoing the buttons of my shirt. One by one. I watch as the wire I am wearing is exposed to her. Her eyes grow big and her mouth falls open.

"You were wearing a wire? Why?"

I pull the thing off and let a grunt slip free when I have to take chest hair with it. "Because now Brad has implicated himself in his own words and you won't have to testify." She looks away and I can tell she hasn't thought that far ahead about what would happen after Brad was arrested.

"So all of the things you told Brad...,? They were just things to make him tell you what he planned and what he's done.

I give her a nod. "For the most part."

Her eyes come back to mine and her body tenses up. "What parts are true? You said for the most part which implies some of it was true."

"The part where you aren't leaving." She sucks in a breath that has her chest rising. My hands drop to my belt and Lacie starts trying to scoot further back - away from me.

"Erik, please." I don't know if she is aware of what she is asking for. I don't think she is. I think she is scared of what happened and still worried I might be like Brad.

"Please what, baby? Please eat this little pussy for you until you cover my mouth and drip down my chin? Please make you scream with how good I am going to give it to you. Please hurry? What please do you want Lacie?"

My pants hit the floor and instead of crawling onto the bed with her and leading her into the sweet lovemaking I wanted to give her for her first time, I remain standing. That was before she ran from me. That was before I thought I was going to lose her. I push her legs apart and fall to my knees in front of her. I bite down on the hand covering her, keeping me from looking at her little pussy. She yelps and jerks her hand away. I take the opportunity to replace it with my mouth.

Her body goes stiff before melting into the bed. Her pussy is already wet and I wonder if she got off on me carrying her up the stairs or does my body do that for her? Maybe the thought of all that I want to do to her makes her body ready itself for me. Whatever it is I lick up all the cream that is there.

She looks at me with worried eyes. Her legs hanging over my shoulders tense up with each lick, pulling me further into her.

"Erik, I don't know..." I cut her off by spearing my tongue into her tight little hole, causing her to arch off the bed and cry out. I don't give her a chance to catch her breath as I slip one of my fingers inside her. She had trouble taking my pinkie last time but this time I can push my middle finger inside with some work. It doesn't hurt that she is so wet, and-drenched.

She's moaning and the arm around her breasts has dropped giving me an excellent view of her cherry-tipped mounds.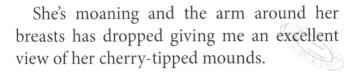

"Oh sweet fuck, Erik!" her body explodes around my hand. Her pussy sucking at my finger as her hands land on her breasts and squeezes them much harder than I would have if I was playing with them. Damn it's sexy to watch though. I don't give her a moment of rest as I build her up to another release. Her hips move of their own accord now, back and forth against my lips. I make sure I lick up every bit of what she just gave me.

"Give me more, Lacie." It's not really a statement so much as a command. And she follows orders beautifully as her body shakes and thrusts through another orgasm. This one isn't as big as the last one but it still rings every bit of energy out of her until her body is left lying limp and sated under me. I move up her body and take her lips in a kiss.

She willingly turns to me and offers her mouth. I know she can taste herself on my lips and tongue and it's sexy as hell. The tip of my cock nudges her sensitive pussy and she makes a sound that I swallow up in my kiss. I push against her until the head is lodged just inside of her. If I wanted to I could take her innocence with one good push. It's tempting but more than anything I want to make sure I can feel every part of her as I open her up for my cock and mine alone.

I pull my mouth away from her so I can stare into her dark eyes as I push further inside of her. Her sweet body gives under the pressure and it doesn't take long until I am right up against her hymen. Lacie sucks in a breath and I watch as her eyes go round. Her hands come up to grab my shoulders. I flex my hips and the thin barrier snaps. Lacie whimpers and moisture gathers at the corners of her eyes. When it spills over I bend to lick it up, even her pain tastes good to me.

Chapter 3

Lacie

He doesn't move inside me. I thought the way he just kind of barged into me that he would be thrusting in and out without a care in the world, especially not my pain. I should have known better. Erik is nothing like what I've expected right from the beginning. He's nothing like my stepfather. I can tell by the tick of his jaw that it'snot easy for him to hold still but he is - for me. Just like he put himself in the line of fire and wore a wire instead of having me go through the ordeal of testifying.

I hadn't even thought that far ahead, to the courtroom and the media that would pick up on something so salacious as a step-parent selling their child to one of their friends. Erik had and he did something that he didn't have to so I wouldn't have to go through any of that. Now he's holding still so he doesn't hurt me more than he has to and in turn making himself uncomfortable. It makes me want to do something for him; something of equal value for all that he has done for me. I even understand now why he didn't want me to know that Brad was in the house.

"You...you can move now if you want to." I wiggle my hips a little bit to show him I'm not in as much pain as I was when his thick cock broke through my cherry. I lay my hand on his cheek to have more of that connection with him. It's the first time I have ever felt this close to another person. It feels like he has something inside of him that completes what's inside of me.

"Can I now?" He tests the idea out by rocking his hips back and forth. His eyes are on me and I can tell that if I show even the slightest bit of pain he is going to stop again. But it'snot painful. Pain is the last thing I'm feeling. The way he's sliding in and out of meis making my body come alive in a way I didn't think was possible. Even with his mouth, it wasn't this good.

I let a moan slip from my mouth and his connects with it to eat the sound before it's released into the room.

"Fuck!" he pulls out and I want to cry. I don't want this to be over but maybe it should be. I'm not on anything and he went inside of me without a condom. Maybe he pulled out because he realized and he can go find one. Instead, he stands and pulls me to the side of the bed. He throws my leg over his shoulder turning my body so that it's more open to him. His cock nudges my entrance again and both of us moan when he pops in. "You feel too fucking good, Lacie. You're going to cause me to cum too quickly."

Oh, God. His words make me so hot but also drive home the fact that he can't cum inside me. His hips aren't taking it easy on me anymore and it's so hard for me to tell him he is going to have to stop when it feels so good. His thumb lands on my clit, rubbing while his other hand grips my thigh to him. "Erik...you...can't cum in...oh, God that feels so good."

The way he is working my body is driving me out of my mind. I can tell I'm about to cum again because of how tense my thighs are becoming, the shake that happens just before I lose control of myself is more pronounced.

"You can't cum inside of me. You have to pull out." I finally get out what I have to say but he doesn't act like he hears me. He doesn't slow down or let my thigh go. If anything my words have caused him to speed up. "You can't cum inside of me, Erik. You know I'm not on anything."

"I know." The look that crosses his face is one of pure temptation. He looks like the devil, the kind that makes you really want to give your soul over - no payment necessary. "I'm not pulling out, Lacie."

My mind is trailing behind where it should be. It takes me a second to actually process what he said. What the fuck? I try to pull back away from him but he won't let me.

"Erik, please. If you cum inside of me there's a good chance you'll get me pregnant. You have to pull out."

"I don't. I don't have to do anything I don't want to, Lacie. You're stepdad sold you to me. I'm going to do exactly what he wanted me to do to you."

My traitorous body isn't on board with my brain which is having a small panic attack.

My body is still responding to him. "No, you can't! Please, Erik, pull out!"

"What's the matter, Lacie? Upset that you are going to be my personal breeding mare. I'm going to dump so much cum inside of your little body that there won't be any doubt that you will be knocked up by the end of the night."

"What!? No, you can't! I can't have a baby. I can't take care of a baby. Please!" my words just make him move faster and thrust deeper into my willing body. I can feel my body ready itself to receive what he gives me.

"Guess what the doctor told me, Lacie? He said you're ovulating. He said if I cum inside of you right now it will take root inside that fertile little body of yours and you'll be walking around big and round with my baby growing inside of you. Then you won't be able to run from me, will you, baby."

My mouth drops open. I can't believe what he is telling me. What the hell? I amp up my efforts to pull away from him. I need to think about what he is saying. What all of this means. I can't think straight when he's inside me.

"You jerk, I can't get pregnant now. I don't even have a place to live, how am I going to raise a baby? Wait," A horrible thought pierces the fog of my lust-drenched mind. "You aren't taking it away from me. Were you telling the truth when you said you were going to get me pregnant and take the baby?"

"Fuck no; I'm taking both of you! You aren't going anywhere, Lacie. You belong to me. You have from the moment I slid my fingers inside that warm pussy. Don't even try to pretend you didn't understand this was going to end just like this."

I want to shout at him and tell him he's wrong but my body chooses that moment to give him what he wants. It's the combination of his thumb strumming over my clit and the feel of his cock hitting something deep inside of me that makes it impossible to fight against him. All I can do is hold on. Hold on to his wrists, to the sheets, to my own body as he keeps my climax drawn out.

"That's it, baby. That's it. Give it to me, Lacie. Let me feel you milk the cum from my balls."

Oh God, his words, things I would normally find so dirty and hate, make me want to cum again and again. My body convulses around him and the fire sweeping through me takes the last little bit of good sense I have until all I am left with is him - his face above me, his body inside of mine, his name whispered over and over again from my lips. I feel the moment he cums, the warmth of his seed shoots inside of me and fills me up. There is no undoing this. What he did makes it impossible for either of us to go back again.

His weight pushes me into the mattress until I think I might not be able to take my next breath. My body doesn't mind at all but my brain is in overdrive thinking about what happened between the two of us. What all of his words mean and what the consequences are going to be has my mind spinning.

He finally pulls away from me and slips out leaving me in a puddle of wetness. I think I am too stunned to be fully aware of what he is doing or where he's going because it's not until he is standing in front of me again with a washcloth in his hand that I realize he must have gone to the bathroom.

I sit up gingerly testing how sore the muscles that have never had a workout will be. His hand pushes me back down until I am once more staring at the ceiling.

"Don't get up. It will cause all the cum to fall out of you." He reaches for a pillow and folds it in half before lifting me and shoving it under my hips. He spreads my thighs and I gasp at the first touch of the cloth on the insides of my thighs. "Are you sore? In pain? Tell me if you hurt?"

"I...," I try to make words come but all that happens is a huge sob comes out instead. Oh my God! I don't know what I'm going to do. My life has been in turmoil for over a year now and the further I look ahead all I see is more. His hand stops moving. His stillness causes me to look up and finally meet his eyes. He swipes my thighs with his fingers and holds them up for me to see. His fingers are streaked in cum and blood.

"See this, Lacie." He waits for me to give him a nod. "This means you are mine. It means nobody is ever going to hurt you again. This means you don't have to wonder if you're safe or taken care of ever again. You and our baby will never have to worry about anything, ever." His hand lands on the lower part of my stomach. It's warm and leaves a funny feeling coursing through my body.

"I'm scared." I have to whisper because I'm not strong enough to say it out loud.

"That's why I'm here." He bends down over me so that our faces are closer. "To make sure you are safe and taken care of and you never have to be afraid of anything. Let me do my job and take care of you, baby."

He stares into my eyes for so long and finally, I give him a nod. He gives my mouth a peck before straightening back up and continuing to clean me. One swipe between my puffy lips and I can tell I am still over-stimulated down there. His eyes track my every gasp and sigh so his hand stills almost immediately. "Sore?"

"Sensitive."

"We can work with sensitive, but if you're sore you best let me know. Yes."

I give him a nod as his thumb glides over the swollen bundle of nerves at the top of my sex. Without thinking my hips rise up off the pillow seeking more of his touch. He throws the washcloth over his shoulder before going back to rubbing me some more. I don't even try to hold in the moans and sighs that spill out of my mouth this time.

My body is starting to shudder with another orgasm when the tip of his cock nudges my entrance. He wants to do it again. He wants to have sex with me all over again. His cock slides inside of me this time and even though I am swollen from the first time it still feels good. Better than good. It feels like coming home. Like this is the place I am supposed to be and he's the man I am supposed to be with. He feels like home. Oh my God, what if I lose him like I lost everything else? The thought makes me reach out for him.

"I don't want to go at you too hard this time, Lacie. You're already so pink and swollen from before." His words are interrupted by his own groan of pleasure.

"I don't mind. It feels good. Mmm, so good." I lean my head back so that my body is arched up toward him. He takes the silent invitation I am handing him and latches onto a nipple making my thighs squeeze up around him and causing me to tilt my hips up more. He slides deeper inside me and I moan at the sensations he's causing me to have. His long, thick cock touches nerves I never even knew I had and he keeps hitting a spot that makes my thighs shake with how good and overwhelming it is.

The root of his dick is rubbing against my clit now so every time he drives into me it's like someone is tapping on me there. He's giving me so many new ways to feel good that I think I might die from the pleasure. It certainly feels like I am losing control of everything, my body's movements, my breathing, and my voice. Moans fall from me like that's all I can offer him the longer he keeps deep thrusting into me. Sounds I never thought I would make. I always thought I would be quiet in bed when I was with someone but it sounds like both of us are making a porn movie with how vocal we are. His grunts and my moans are bouncing off the walls and I'm not even worried about anyone else hearing us. All I worry about is getting to that ultimate release again.

"I didn't mean to take you again so soon after you just lost your innocence, baby, but I swear if I stop now I might die. Tell me you aren't hurting. Tell me you're good."

"Oh God, Erik, please don't stop. I'm so close. I'm so close, baby. I...," before I can explain how close to cumming I am I'm already in the middle of my climax. My body seizes up around his and my muscles pulse around the thickness inside of me. He empties himself in me, his cock jerking and throbbing as bad as my pussy is. This time he doesn't leave my body but flips us so that I am lying across his chest and his cock is still inside of me.

I drift off not thinking about the fact that we could have made a baby or the shit storm that is going to happen when the media gets hold of the story that is Brad. I don't worry about not having a home or any place to go. I don't think about anything bad or wrong, all I think about is Erik under me and the sound of his soft breathing as I close my eyes for the last time.

Chapter 7

Lacie

The morning light is coming in from a split in the curtains and giving me hell. I can't go back to the dreams I was having and I don't want to wake up just yet. In my dreams, I'm someone else, wiser, more desirable, not such a hot mess. Erik wants me. Erik uses my body to find his release. I definitely want to stay in my dream for just a little while longer. I roll to my back and feel the collected wetness between my legs. My muscles ache and my pussy is still slightly swollen.

As the fact that I had sex last night sets in, it forces me to sit up in the middle of an empty bed. Where's Erik? Why did he leave? Oh God, I hope I wasn't a one-night stand kind of thing and now he's done with me. I've never woken up naked in a stranger's bed before. Not that Erik is a total stranger. I know a lot about him. I know that he is sweet and kind and he thinks of me and takes care of me more than anyone else has ever done in my life.

A soft knock on the door has me diving back under the covers and not wanting to come out. It doesn't matter who it is. I'm not ready to speak to anyone just yet. A soft voice speaks through the door.

"Are you up? May I come in?"

Oh shit! "Um," my eyes are trying to take in anything I might be able to use as clothing. When they land on one of Erik's shirts thrown over the back of a chair I decide to make a run for it. "Give me just a second, please."

I don't recognize the voice. I know it isn't Dasha. I fumble with the buttons until I finally have them all done up right and then walk to the door on my tippy toes. Maybe this is a maid that comes in and helps Dasha with things and she just wants to clean the room so she can go about the rest of her day.

When I open the door the smile I was working up vanishes. This woman is not a maid, nor does she work for Erik. The strong resemblance between the two tells me just exactly who this woman is. She's his mother. I am standing in her son's room wearing his shirt looking like I had a night of hard fucks - and he is leaking out of me, sliding slowly down the inside of my thighs. This is not the way anyone wants to meet the parents of the people they...fuck? Make love to? Are with intimately? I don't even have a good name for what to call what me and Erik are doing.

The woman is so put together and perfect that it highlights the fact I am a walking mess even more. Her hair is put up in this perfect French knot and her clothes are...well, real clothes and not someone else's shirt. She smells good too and it makes me really worry about what I smell like right now. I didn't have a chance to brush my teeth, or hair for that matter before I opened the door. I am one hundred percent sure she can tell I have slept with her son.

"Hi, I'm Evangeline but everyone calls me Angie." She holds out her hand for me to shake. I automatically give her mine even though I am super aware of our differences in every way.

"I'm...," my voice is soft and thready when it comes out.

"Oh, I know who you are. You don't have

to tell me. I am so happy to finally meet you, Lacie." She knows my name.

"Finally?" That's an odd way of putting it since I've only been here for two days.

"The woman who is going to take down my son, whip him into submission, and give me grandbabies. I've been waiting ages for this moment. Now tell me all about how you and Erik met."

Oh God am I in trouble.

She picks up on my discomfort immediately. "Don't worry. Dasha told me everything already. She explained all about what was going on with your stepfather." Her smile melts off her face and her brows crease in the middle of her eyes. "I can't believe a father would do that to his child, even a stepchild. And you being so tiny must have been scared to death when Erik does his damned towering-over-you thing. I hate it and I have a good couple of inches on you."

I'm not sure if I should be upset or embarrassed that this woman knows I was given away like a cheap trinket in a poker game. It's not something I really want to shout from the rooftops but it also wasn't my fault that any of it happened. I definitely know I don't want to be known as the girl Erik won in a bet.

"Come have breakfast with me and tell me all about yourself. You look young. Please tell me you're eighteen."

My eyes round and I quickly nod my head. She takes me by the hand and pulls me out of the safety of Erik's bedroom before I can say anything else.

"Oh good. I don't think if Erik wants you age would be enough to stop him and from what Dasha says he more than wants you." Her eyes run up and down me before breaking out into a big grin.

I'm down the stairs and in the kitchen before I can think of a reason not to go with her. She stands at the stove after having sat me at the island that resides in the middle of the room. I don't ask what she's making. I'm too concerned with what's coming out of my mouth to worry about what will go in it.

"So tell me what you think of Erik. I hope my boy has made a good impression so far."

Her words make me think of yesterday and how he took me over. How demanding he was and how he told me he was going to put a baby in me makes me shift on the seat and I can tell I am blushing.

"He...is sweet."

"Sweet?" she looks like I am not talking about the same person she is.

"He took care of me. He made sure I wouldn't have to testify in court about what happened. He made me feel safe. He makes me feel safe." I don't think I can bring my eyes up to look at her. What if she tells me how I see Erik is not the real Erik? What then?

"That's part of my job, Lacie." Hands land on my shoulders and cause me to almost fall out of my chair. Cool lips brush against my forehead when I look up at Erik himself standing over me. "To take care of you and keep you safe."

He's looking over the top of my head at his mom who is also looking at him. Some unspoken communication is going on between mother and son but I can't tell what it is.

"Mother, I thought I ask you to give me a

couple of days?"

"Well, I did give you a couple of days. If you wanted a few you should have said a few or maybe several. Words matter, Erik."

Something akin to acceptance crosses Erik's face right before he looks down at me. "When my business started doing better mom was able to quit her day job and start writing. She always wanted to be a writer and it's turned her into something of a smartass."

"Oh honey, I've always been smart I didn't have to change jobs to get that way." Angie throws her head back and laughs at her son and his exasperation.

Dasha comes through the door right at that moment. She was suspiciously absent since we hit the kitchen. She takes in everyone in the room and then holds her hands up in surrender. "I tried to give her enough information to keep her away Erik but the more I gave her the more she wanted to know. Don't blame me for this. This is all you. If you didn't want her here you should have called her and told her about Lacie."

She walks around to stand beside his mom.

"I'm not blaming anyone, Dasha. I would have just liked to introduce you to Lacie myself, Mom. Not to mention she might have liked being dressed for the meeting." His words make my cheeks heat again.

"Don't be silly. She isn't running around naked for God's sake. And I knocked and ask to come in. It wasn't like I let myself in and sat near her bed until she woke up." She turns back around to focus on the food she is making. "Dasha wouldn't let me."

My eyes widen. Oh dear God what would I have done if she had been there when I was waking up to find myself covered in cum. I look at Dasha and catch her eye. I mouth the words thank you and she gives me a big grin before turning back around to help Angie.

Erik bends down low so he is whispering in my ear. "I assume you didn't have time to take a shower or bath?" I shake my head. "Good. You still have me inside of you then."

I gasp loud enough to make the two women turn around and look at us. Angie's eyes light up when she sees her son slide into the seat beside my own. He's so big he takes up more room than I do especially when he is sitting like he is now - sideways. He grabs my chair by the leg and scoots it closer so that I am in between his legs. One of his hands lands on my ass while the other one rests on my thigh. He nuzzles into the crook of my shoulder and I can't stop the laugh that bubbles out of me at the breath of air that fans across my neck tickling me.

"Mom is going to have just enough time to feed you and then your mine again."

My mouth falls open and my eyes shoot to his mom who is still looking at us. Erik wasn't quiet when he said what he said so I have no doubt that his mom heard him. As if reading my mind he also looks over at his mom. "Mom if you want grandchildren I suggest you hurry."

All the blood drains out of my head but Angie laughs again and turns back to the stove. "Come on Dasha, we got to get these crepes made and on a plate asap."

Erik's phone rings and he excuses himself so he can take it. When he goes his mom turns back around to me and leaves the stove to Dasha.

"He's never been like this before. It makes me so happy to see him this way."

"He's not like what?" I really want to understand why his mom and Dasha are making such a fuss. Is it just because Angie wants babies? Or is it really a huge change for Erik and they are happy about it?

"So...," she pauses to think about the right word.

"Affectionate." Dasha supplies for her.

"Yes. That's it. Erik is always so serious and hardly ever smiles but when he's with you he seems to be smiling all the time. He doesn't mind showing his affection for you to me and Dasha and I bet he won't stop with us. I bet he'll show you love no matter who's around." Her mention of the 'L' word my eyes round. "He doesn't even seem all caught up in his work like he used to be."

I am about to ask about his work when he walks back in. Is he going to be a workaholic? I understand that his mom says he is different with me but what happens if he starts working like that again? Will I be left at home with a baby and nannies and no husband? Can I live with that? What the hell am I going to do with myself while he works? I don't think I can stomach spending my days shopping and being a society wife. Is that the kind of wife he wants me to be? Does he even want me to be his wife? I guess I just assumed with all his talking about me being his and only his that he would want to marry me but maybe I'm wrong? It's not like we have spent a lot of time talking.

Erik surprises me again when he comes back into the room. This time though he doesn't sit in the chair next to me but lifts me out of mine and sits me in his lap. He nuzzles into me again. "What's on your mind, baby?"

"How do you know anything is on my mind?"

"You have a line between your brows and you're chewing on your lips like they might end up breakfast instead of the crepes."

"I just...," I look over at his mom and Dasha. For once they are consumed with making breakfast and not watching us. "I was wondering what happens now. What exactly do you expect from me?"

"I expect you to stay with me. Other than that, everything else will come or it won't."

"But what does that mean? Am I... your girlfriend? Your live-in lover? Your...," I stop short of saying the word fiancé.

"Mmm, you are my lover," he places a kiss on my neck just below my ear, "you are the mother of my future children," another kiss follows his words, "you will be my wife, and you are most definitely going to be staying with me before we get married so yes you will be living with me."

He stands up and takes me with him. "Mom, keep the food hot." He turns around with me in his arms and starts heading back to the bedroom.

"Where are we going?"

"We are going somewhere we can talk without being overheard or having a rapt audience so we can say things we need to say to one another."

As soon as we are inside he uses his foot to push the door closed and then lays me on the bed, coming over me. His hands go for the buttons of the shirt. "This doesn't look like we will be doing much talking."

"We can talk without wearing clothes."

His fingers make quick work of them before he slides the shirt off my shoulders. "You want me to define what you are to me?" I nod. It is something I need to have answered. "From the moment I saw you I knew you were mine. I wasn't ever going to let you leave me. I wanted you then. I desired your body. I lusted after you. Then you opened those beautiful brown eyes and gave me your trust. I got to meet the person behind the body. And I got to experience what it is like to be given that complete trust over your body and your heart and I fell in love with you."

Oh my God! He used the 'L' word.

"When I walked into the kitchen to rescue you from my mother and heard how you talked about me and what you thought about me I only fell deeper. Being without you for even a little while is painful and all I can think about is the next time I can touch you or talk to you or even see you again. You consume my mind and have completely taken over my heart. Does that answer your question?"

All I can do is shake my head. Tears are standing in my eyes. No one has ever said something so sweet to me or made me feel like I was needed. "I love you too. I thought maybe you might want just a baby and I would be, I don't know, left at home all day doing nothing. Being nothing. Other than something pretty to put on your arm when you needed me. I don't know if I can live that kind of life, Erik. I'm not...whatever it is you need. I'm messy and goofy and I would spend all my time worrying about fucking this up between you and me."

His lips come down on mine cutting my words off. The kiss is long and deep and makes me forget about everything but his lips on mine. His hands glide up my sides causing me to gasp through the kiss. His touch is magic; it calms me like nothing else ever could. My fears melt away when he's with me.

"I don't care what you want to be. Whatever it is will be exactly what I want because I just want you, as messy and crazy as you can be. And I am working on taking more time off so I can spend it with you and if we have a baby I'll be able to spend it with both of you. It might take me a while to get everything where I want it so that I can walk away from it for long periods of time but I've already started putting the plan into place for me to do just that."

"You did?" He nods his head. His smile stretching across his lips has my heart beating faster and faster. "When?"

With all the shit concerning Brad going on I'm not sure when he would have the time to do something like make plans to spend more time with me.

"The first night you were here. That was a long night for me, wondering if you would be okay and how you would react when you woke up. I wanted you to stay and I was worried you would want to leave me because of how we met. I started putting together a plan to take more time away from work so I could make you fall in love with me. The first phase of the plan started today. It was what I was working on when Dasha came and told me Mom was kidnapping you away from me."

I giggle at the way he describes what happened between his mom and me. It was very much like being overtaken by something forceful.

"If you want to go to school you can, if you want to focus on being a mom full time you can, if you want to start your own business you can. There is nothing you can't do and I will be by your side the entire way."

The thought of school makes my chest hurt. Mom would want me to go to college and that's what the money from her should have gone to. I don't think she would have faulted me for using it to get away from Brad but I never got further than getting somewhere I could feel safe again when I planned my future.

"I would like to start a family soon but if you aren't already pregnant and you want to wait we can." I can hear in his voice how much he wants a family with me. I want that too. "I know I was a little...pushy about starting one last night but I want you to understand we are partners in everything, even deciding when and if we start our family. Especially that."

"I want a family with you. I want to show a child what it's like to have a loving home with two people who love one another and work together to make something good out of their lives."

His smile is the only reward I would ever need for telling him one of my secret wishes. I never told anyone about actually wanting a family and what that would be like to have to give to a child. I felt like it was something I couldn't have before Erik. Hell, before Erik I didn't even know if I wanted to have sex with another human being so no way was I going to jump in and start making a family with just anyone.

He holds my head in his hands, "So let's practice making a baby." His smile falters, "Unless you're too sore. I wanted to let you sleep in this morning and come wake you up slowly and then let you get your bath that got cut short yesterday but Mom had other plans."

"I'm not sore."

Tender maybe but not sore, especially not too sore for more of him. More of his time and attention. More of the mind-blowing orgasms he gives me. More of the love I feel when he is buried deep inside of me.

Chapter 8

Erik

As soon as she tells me she's not too sore to make love to me again I set out to slowly ease into her again. She's all I could think about this morning. I know she must be sensitive from all the things I did to her the day before. It hasn't been twenty-four hours since she lost her virginity. I run my hands down the insides of her thighs and pull her apart so I can see how red and puffy she is. It's my job to make sure she doesn't hurt herself just because she wants something. If she is too tender I will just have to eat her pretty little pussy until she cums and then teach her how to give me a blow job.

I pull her puffy folds apart and stare at her creamy center. She's so wet, so ready for me, it makes it hard to think about anything else. I had to leave her alone this morning or I was going to slide my dick back inside of her and she needed to rest. The only way I could fight the temptation was to go to another room. I hated leaving her though.

I could still taste her and smell her on me when I went to my office and I couldn't start my day until I took my cock out and drained it while thinking about her in our bed, lying so wet and ready for me. I meant what I said when I told her I wanted her to wake up slowly and easily and have a bath first thing. There is no way I want to make her too tender to make love to me later.

Her little pussy is still swollen but so fucking wet. I run my finger up the middle and pop it into my mouth to suck the cream off. God, having the flavor of her on my tongue is something I am going to be addicted to. Thank God I own my own business so I can keep her close no matter where I'm at. I have every intention of taking her to work with me when I have to go in again.

"Sore?" I ask her again and watch her face when I run my finger back up the middle of her sweet tight pussy. She shakes her head and I don't see her flinch or show any sign that she is hurting. "If it starts to hurt you tell me. Right away, don't hesitate because you think I won't finish you. I'll still get you off even if I can't do it with my cock, baby."

She nods but her hips rise off the bed in an invitation I am not about to turn down. My mouth is on her sweet flesh before she can take her next breath. I will never make my woman beg for it - unless we are playing that kind of game and she wants me to. I run my tongue down the same alley my finger took before. She lets out a cute as fuck little squeal before it turns into a moan as my tongue starts flicking the bud of her clit back and forth. I apply pressure and her hips start rocking up and down.

My hands slide to her breasts and start rubbing her nipples with the same gentle rhythm I am tongue-rubbing her clit with.

"Oh God, that's so good! Oh, how does it just keep getting better and better every time?" I would answer her or at least try, but I am too busy chasing down all of her cream. It leaks from her body with every lash of my tongue and I want more. "Oh yes, oh God, yes baby. Please make me cum. Oh, I'm so close. Please, please don't stop."

I start sucking her little nub into my mouth. I want something of me inside of her when she cums and she's close I can tell. Even if it's just my finger I want to feel her contract around me and know that she is preparing her little body for me to breed her. I glide two fingers inside of her. It's a tight fit even though she had my huge cock inside of her not too long ago. It's going to take some time to really break her in and make it easy for me to push my dick inside of her sweet body. I curl my fingers up inside of her right on the bundle of nerves that will make her go insane. It doesn't take long after I find it and start playing with it that she quivers around my digits and floods my mouth with her sexy juices. I could live off of eating her.

I crawl up her body before the last of her high has worn off. Her eyes are still dazed and she has a big happy smile on her face that I hope I can keep there for the rest of our lives. There are so many ways I want to take her. So many things I want to do with her. It is hard to pick which one I want to do first. I can't wait until she tells me which one she likes and which ones she wants to do again.

I push my cock inside of her still lightly fluttering pussy and wait. If I move too fast this will be over before it has begun for me. I waited too long to be inside of her again. Having her squeeze up around me is both painful and pleasure like no other. I want to last long enough to make her body come apart for me, to watch as I fuck her so hard her tits bounce with every thrust.

I throw her legs up over my shoulders so I can go deep inside, the tip of my cock touching the mouth of her cervix. Fuck. I'm not going to last. I start rubbing her hard little nub to make sure she cums with me. Her hips arch off the bed as she starts to spasm around me. I lose my hold on her thighs and her legs go from around my neck to wrapped around my waist. Her nails drag down my arms as the heels of her feet push into the cheeks of my ass so that she can hold me to her when she cums. She doesn't have to hold me, I'm not going anywhere.

Her body brushes against mine and I release inside of her giving her what she wants. She falls back on the bed still holding me to her. Even though both of us are exhausted and she must be starving I take my time moving. Instead, I slide down, my cock leaving her body in a slippery glide and rest my head on her breasts so I can hear her heart beating. Her hands lazily run through my hair and down my back causing me to shiver for her. She might not understand it yet but she has all the control in this relationship. I would give her anything, do anything for her, and protect and love her for as long as I live.

"If we don't go downstairs soon your mom is going to come looking for us." I look up at her and see the grin on her face and the mischief in her eyes.

"Please, she is probably right outside the door now waiting to see if you feel pregnant or not." She laughs out loud at that but I'm not joking. Mom has been waiting a long time for this. Who would have thought I would find love with someone I won in a hand of poker? But Lacie is the best ante I have ever bet on. Who knew when I was winning that bet that I was really betting on love - and I won more than I ever thought I could.

Epilogue 1

Lacie

I am supposed to be getting married today. His mom and Dasha have invited more people than I have ever seen in a room at one time. Almost all of the people that work for Erik are here and my friends from school. I cannot be sick today of all days. Why in the hell couldn't this virus wait until at least twenty-four hours when I would be sitting with my husband in a private cabana on the beach? I mean it would suck being sick at the beach but at least I wouldn't run the risk of getting sick in front of all these people.

I've already thrown up once today and I felt like shit this morning when I got up. A small knock on the door of the room I'm in jolts me out of my thoughts and back into the present. "Come in."

Angie takes one look at me and her eyes light up with glee. What the hell? I'm not sure why she would be so happy about me being sick but she looks like she is going to pop a button she's so excited. She runs back out leaving the door open wide. I just want to curl up on the couch and hide - and maybe nap. A nap sounds good.

She's back a moment later digging in her purse. She doesn't say a word just hands me a box with a bunch of pink on it and hops from foot to foot. I look down and read the front. My eyes widen and shoot to her. "Did you get this out of your purse?" She gives me an excited nod. "Do you carry them around with you all the time?"

"Oh honey, I have them stashed everywhere. I knew as much as you and my Erik were going at it you would need one sooner rather than later and as your maternal figure, I was not about to let you down when this moment came. Now go pee on that stick and let's see if we have a little bundle on the way."

"Shouldn't we wait for Eric or some...", Eric comes sliding into the room with his hair all messed up and his breath coming in ragged pants.

"You're not supposed to see me before the wedding!" I turn to Angie, "Right?"

"That only counts if you're in your dress dear. The robe should be perfectly fine."

"No way in hell am I missing this. Mom texted saying you think you might be...," he doesn't finish. He's been counting down the days until I missed a period. I don't know who is more excited about this him or his mom... or me. I'm just nervous and nauseous too.

Eric knows how sick I was this morning. He actually got up with me to help pick me up off the floor when I was done. He wanted to postpone, but I was absolutely not going to put marrying him off...until an hour before and now I think I don't want to vomit on the guests as I walk to my future husband. That would probably be construed as a bad omen.

"You two go, do your thing. I'll wait here. But don't take too long dear."

I'm not sure which one of us she is talking to because she calls both of us dear so we both just do what she says and I walk into the bathroom with Erik. He shuts the door and gives me some space to do my business without him watching and making it too weird. Then I wash my hands as we both wait for the test to show us if we are going to have a baby or a hospital visit on our hands.

Time feels like it is dragging and I look at the damned stick a hundred times before the three minutes is up. Erik finally wraps his arms around me and distracts me by kissing me until the timer on my phone goes off. We both hesitate. Both of us want to find out what the thing has to tell us but both of us are nervous it won't tell us what we want it to either. Finally, a rap on the door has us jumping into action.

"Tell me already, I heard the timer go off in there. Do you know yet?" Angie is just as anxious and excited.

I stare down at the stick on the counter and the two lines staring back at me. Two lines. That means...Erik grabs me and kisses me with so much happiness and passion that it is hard to keep thinking about things like weddings and Angie and babies. He ends the kiss way too soon and throws the door open.

"I'm a Daddy!"

Angie bursts into tears and runs to hug and kiss me while Dasha who must have shown up while we were in the bathroom gives Erik a hug. She hands Angie a brown paper bag. Angie takes out the box and hands it to me. Ginger suckers.

"They're supposed to be really good for upset tummies. I have a friend who is an Ob/Gyn and she swears by them. Maybe they will help. Just to get us through the next couple of hours until we can figure something else out. After all, you have a wedding to be at and a man to marry. Here dear let me fix your makeup and Dasha can fix your hair." She looks over at her son, "Leave so we can get this show on the road."

"Can you give me a minute with the mother of my children please?" It's not really a question even though he asks it like one.

Both women chuckle and make a run for the door.

Erik comes over to me and wraps me in his arms. "Have I told you how lucky I am to have you? How thankful I am that you were the ante?"

"Hmm, not in the last couple of hours."

"Then I should remedy that, my beautiful bride." He undoes the sash on my robe and it slithers off my shoulders and lands on the floor. "Do you think you're well enough to have this sweet little pussy eaten before we say 'I do'?"

"Oh yeah, I think that might help settle my stomach better than anything else could."

We're thirty minutes late to our own wedding and I walk down the aisle with Erik's cum still dripping out of me. But my fear of vomiting on the guest is a distant memory.

Epilogue 2

Erik
Ten Years Later

My lovely wife is helping our little girl find her feet after being knocked off of them by a wave. The family is at the beach for the weekend. School starts back soon for the other three and the twins and we won't have as much time to go on family outings. Not that it means we won't have time for each other. Lacie and I are a part of the kids school in almost every aspect there can be, I even sit on the board.

I very rarely go into the office anymore. I still run the business, just remotely and I have a lot of good people working for me making it possible for me to take more time for my family. Lacie looks more beautiful than she did the day I meet her. Her body has filled out; her curves are rounder and her breasts bigger. I love sucking her milk-filled tits. It's one of the reasons we've had so many children and I keep knocking her up but Abby is our last. Six healthy children are more of a blessing than I ever thought I would be allowed.

Brad finally got what was coming to him. Turns out Lacie and her mom weren't the first time Brad tried to do something awful to someone and when he went to jail he was found hanging in his cell about two weeks before the trial. Lacie looked at me like I might have had something to do with it but I promise I didn't this time. I wanted him to face prison time for what he had done to her. One of the four other families of the people he had harmed didn't agree with me and so they suspect one of them had him killed. He's just a distant memory to us now.

Lacie comes over and hands Abby over to Rachel, our oldest, who plays quietly with her in the sand. She drops a kiss on my head before sitting in the chair next to me. "You're mom just text. She and Dasha have dinner ready whenever we are ready to come in."

"Maybe Mom can watch the little ones for us for a little while after dinner and we can sneak away back out here when it's dark and quiet."

"Hmm, sounds good. How about your

mom watches them for a little while before dinner too? I'm sure grandma can supervise clean up before dinner."

"Kids'! Let's go, everyone in, supper's almost ready." I shout to all of my children making sure to count them as they troop by us and up the sandy hill to our house where I can already see my Mom waving to them from the back porch.

If anyone asks me how good life could be before I met Lacie I would have had a much different answer than I do now. I pull my wife down into my lap and kiss her soft sweet lips. If they ask me now, I would tell them without thinking - You Bet!

The End!!

Keep reading on to catch a glimps of the third installment in the Taboo series, *Sticky Business.*

STICKY BUSINESS

STICKY BUSINESS

Aaron "Pope" Benedict wants revenge and it's the only thing on his mind until he sees Mary. Yeah, pulling Mary into his revenge plot by making her go on a couple's cruise their cheating exs are on is petty and wrong but not as wrong as finding out Mary is a virgin and he just brought her on a wild exhibitionist boat ride and now he can't keep his hands off of her. He might be called 'Pope' but holy he is not and Mary won't be leaving the boat the same way she came aboard. But has his need for vengeance kept him from starting a new life with Mary? And what happens when they reach their destination?

This is a fun, silly taboo tale about a man just wanting to get back at his ex until he sees the other guy's woman. Don't let the synopsis throw you, the two lovers are very much over their exs and looking to move on. It's hot and summery and sticky and isn't that something we all need more of!

Aaron

I've been waiting out here for him to leave for work. I don't know much about the girl inside other than she's young. She goes to college and she has a lying sack of shit for a boyfriend. I know more about him but thinking about him makes me angry and I need to keep my cool right now. If I blow this I might not have a chance to seek the kind of revenge I know hurts the most.

I walk up the little stoop in front of their place and knock on the door. I roll my neck hoping to unleash some of the stress I'm feeling. The door opens slightly and I can see the security chain between her and me. Staring up at me is the prettiest set of chocolate eyes I've ever seen. They knock me speechless for a second.

"Can I help you?" her voice is uncertain and I remind myself not everybody knows that I won't rob and kill them. At least not anymore.

I know what I look like. I'm not 'pretty'. I have scars covering a good part of my body and the rest is covered in tattoos. I'm not muscle man built but I'm not built like her boyfriend either. To look at me someone would think I am about to do bad things to this little thing. Someone should tell her that a security chain isn't going to do her a damn bit of good if a man like me wants to come in.

I could have the door opened and be on top of her before she has time to realize there is a problem but I don't do that. I never did that. I was always more of the victimless crime kind of guy. I stole shit, I fucked some people up but they were bad people so they don't count, and I may have sold some shit that wasn't quite legal yet. Nothing like the thoughts going through my fucking head now. I can only blame the fucker for making me angry and leading my mind down the path of revenge-seeking.

"You don't know me ma'am but I know your boyfriend."

"David?" she doesn't believe me. At least she's smart enough to not trust me. I nod and pull at my hoodie under my jacket.

"Yeah, David." Shit, I can't keep the hate out of my voice. "Can I come in?"

She looks behind her for a second and then gives me those melty brown eyes back again. "Now's not a good time. Can you come back, maybe later?"

"Look ma'am, I'm not trying to scare the shit out of you or anything but I know you're in there alone, and what I have to say needs to be said between me and you."

Fear hits her eyes and for the first time in a long fucking time my cock grows. Thank God I have some layers to hide my erection behind.

"David's cheating on you with my girlfriend." After I say the words I want to snatch them back up again. Fear is one thing but the pain I see now guts me. "I have evidence if you want to see and I just want to talk to you. I thought you should know too."

Her eyes have left me and I feel like I've fucking lost something. When they look back up at me they are swimming in unshed tears. She closes the door quietly and I hear her messing with the chain before she opens the door back up again. She opens it wide enough that I can come in but I don't move until she gives me the go-ahead. Her head nods to indicate she wants me to come inside.

She turns to lead me into the living room and my eyes fall on her ass. It's wrapped in soft, cotton sleep shorts that hug her cheeks like they are thankful they are there. It's been a long time since I've had sex but damn I have to get myself under control here. She waves me to a couch before taking a chair beside me and curling her bare feet up under her. She's in a tank top that stretches across young, firm-looking tits that are too big for her frame.

"You said you have evidence."

I scoot forward and take my phone from my pocket. I already have the video cued up. I hit the button as I scoot even closer to her chair. I've watched this at least a hundred times. At first, I wanted to kill them but I'm not throwing away my second chance by murdering two pieces of shit that don't matter in the end. The video shows her boyfriend walking up to my girlfriend, Shelia's car, a car I bought her. He gets in and before too long they are kissing. Then Shelia crawls over the shifter to straddle

David and the two of them start fucking. It's pretty in your face and obvious that's what's happening. I mean the two of them are both grunting and sweating and Shelia keeps moving up and down on David's cock.

She pushes the phone away before it ends. I pause the video. More happens but I don't think she wants to watch anymore. I look up and silent tears are running down her cheeks. Silence hangs heavy between the two of us for a long second.

"I'm sorry."

Her apology makes me furious. Not being able to sit anymore I stand and start to pace back and forth. "Why are you sorry? You weren't fucking David, Shelia was."

She lets out a strangled noise like I slapped her and I dial back the anger. I go to her and go down on my knees in front of her chair. "Look, I need your help. We've both been fucked over by people we thought we could trust." I don't use the word love on purpose. She might have loved David but for me, Shelia was just something, an idea, I wanted; didn't matter if it was her or someone else.

She runs her hand up to fiddle with the strap of her tank and my eyes are riveted to her. I got to get this shit under control or she's going to ruin everything.

"David's going away on a business trip next week right?" she nods. "Wrong. He and Shelia booked a week-long vacation together on a couple's cruise." I show her the picture I took of the flyer. It's the Midnight Embrace cruise. It has a whole bunch of romantic shit and at the end, they take you to a small island in the Caribbean so you can 'make love in the sand with the moon as your only light'. I nearly fucking gagged as I was reading it.

"Why are you showing me this? How does this have anything to do with how I can help you?"

"Because I booked a cabin on the same cruise. I want to catch them in the act and I want to embarrass the shit out of them in front of their peers. I want them to think me and you are fucking so they understand how bad it feels. I want them to have to think about why we would choose each other over them."

She started shaking her head right after I mentioned making them think we were fucking each other. "I can't help you."

I knew the whole making them jealous and realize what they had and gave up would be a hard sell but I also wanted to be upfront with her on what I wanted her to do. "I can't get on the boat if I'm alone, couples only. Please just help me onto the boat. If you want to take the sad sack of shit back after we out them then at the very least help me call them out."

"I'm sorry I can't help you. I have to get ready for school." She stands up and I'm at eye level with her hips. A tempting as fuck scent hits my nose and I wonder if it's her pussy. She shuffles around me still on my knees and goes to the front door. She holds it open telling me as nicely as she can without saying any damn thing to get the fuck out. I stand up. Upset as hell that this is how this is going to end with her.

I'm not done. I just have to find someone else to go with me now. Someone who I can tolerate for a whole fucking week. My eyes meet hers as I walk by her to leave.

"Let me ask you something, do you think it's going to be enough for you to know that every time you see him his dick is going to be wet with some other pussy. It's Shelia now but who else will it be in the future, how many people are you sharing a bed with?"

"Go! Now!" her eyes won't meet mine anymore. I pull one of my cards from the inside pocket of my jacket and hand it to her.

"Think about what I said and if you want some justice, call me." I don't move any farther out the door and I won't until she takes my card. She snatches it out of my hand but doesn't look at it.

We never told each other our names, we didn't have a chance to talk about anything other than the asshats who caused us so much pain, and I didn't get to see her smile. I feel like my whole fucking day is wasted and I'm blaming the cheating shits who put me in this situation.

I flip my collar up and take off down the street. Back to my side of town. I'm a long way from where I started. I customize bikes now. Expensive ones that celebrities seem to like. I mess around with classic cars sometoo but that's not really what I'm known for. I get back to the shop and head straight for my office. I've got a whole fucking team of workers under me now but when I started out it was just me and a couple of old broke-down bikes. I slam my office door shut and lock it.

My cock is out in my hands before I can stop myself. I grab it and slide my hand up and down it a couple of times before my balls are starting to tighten up. I cum with images of her in my mind and the memory of that fresh smell that I am sure was her pussy.

Scan below to read *Sticky Business* fully.

ABOUT THE AUTHOR

Jisa Dean has been in love with love since she was four years old. Lover of Gudetama, instalove and happy ever afters. When she's not making herself blush with her writing, she's a mom and wife, constantly wondering how to hide her naughty alter-ego from the PTO moms in the pickup line. She would love nothing more than to spread smut throughout the land - so come get smutty with her!

www.JisaDean.com

Made in the USA
Middletown, DE
11 May 2023